Selections from the
"100 Best" Children's Stories from China

Volume 1

As told by
Dr. Robert Chi-Kwong Lee
& Doreen Lee Ong

Acknowledgements

The authors gratefully acknowledge the contribution of Yang Li for all the excellent illustrations, Kenny and Millie Yamada for coloring the cover illustration and formatting of this book, and our beloved families for their patience and support.

The authors also want to express their appreciation to Mrs. Bernadette Shih for her help and guidance throughout the preparation of this book.

i

Library of Congress Card Number: 00-192681

ISBN: 0-9706876-0-5

To place orders, please visit www.find100best.com or your local bookstore.

For Zoe & Amy

with all the love a heart can hold,
and prayers for hearts as pure as gold...
you are better than 100 Best!

A Note from the Storytellers:

When I was a little girl, one of my favorite activities was to curl up with my father on the patio swing and listen to stories like these as the sunset faded into twilight. Some of them were old Chinese legends, others he invented just for me, but always they were filled with wisdom, love, and creativity. They stirred my imagination, gave me clever, capable role models, and reminded me that I was deeply treasured by my parents -that they loved me and cared about how I grew up.

We hope you and your family enjoy these stories as much as we have, and that together, you create some special memories of your own.

Doreen Lee Ong

Dear parents, grandparents, concerned aunts, uncles and friends:

"A mind is a terrible thing to waste." Everyone accepts this truism and yet if we look around us, we will find that we often are wasting the minds of our children.

How?

First of all, we may use "baby talk" with babies thinking that they do not understand us. Modern research called Neuro-Linguistic Programming (NLP) shows that although a baby does not talk or understand our words, his brain stores up the words we say. A baby's brain is similar to a computer that stores up every bit of data that comes in, but lacks the program to interpret the data. NLP explains that when a baby reaches one to two years of age, his neural networks suddenly begin to connect and he begins to talk. Many a mother has been surprised that her infant has a command of words that she never consciously taught him.

The truth is, a child's brain is like a sponge that absorbs everything that happens around it. The child mimics in her brain every word she has heard. Children learn manners and ethics the same way. That's why parenting is a great responsibility that must be taken seriously. Do you know one reason why there are so many dysfunctional families in the world? The homemakers are not home! By that, I mean, that true "homemakers" are the parents, both male and female, who take the time and energy to invest in the intellectual, social, emotional, moral, and spiritual development of their little ones. We must give our children both quantity and quality time for this important development to take place properly.

Another well-intentioned mistake we make as parents is that we underestimate the intelligence of our children. Sometimes we fill their minds with only the simplest stories and videos, thinking they are too young to handle any deeper thoughts or concepts. In truth, children can comprehend much more than we give them credit for, because the brain is developed well before the body matures. This has been proven by the accomplishments of many young musicians, athletes and scholars.

"My children are just average," some may say. What makes

them average? What makes one think they are average? Do you know Einstein was considered "slow" in his early years? Our job is to help our children realize their maximum potential.

Raising our precious children in a complex world is at best a difficult task. There are so many voices and opinions that one can be easily confused. Just look at the children's TV programs. What do they teach? Are they just mindless entertainment or do they have some specific objectives? Have you watched some of the children's TV shows and games lately? Some are full of anger and violence. Is this really what we want to program into their minds?

We at 100 Best believe that our children's minds must be challenged. Just like muscles, they need to be stretched and exercised to go beyond their normal limits. They need to be constantly stimulated, challenged and at the same time be instilled with a firm value system. Children always mimic their parents. Let us provide them with a good model to follow.

This book is written to be read by older children, perhaps

grade 4 and up, or to be read and interpreted by parents for their little ones.

The stories in this book were chosen in order to give children in our Western culture a better understanding of the Asian mind. Many of these stories are ages old; they have been told and retold for hundreds or even thousands of years. Some are relatively new. Each was chosen based on the following criteria.

We chose stories that are interesting and imaginative, educational (containing new words, new facts, new thoughts), stimulating and challenging to young minds. Furthermore, we chose them for an inherent value lesson and also to provide an opportunity to stimulate conversation, whereby the adult may guide the child.

Each story ends with a "treasure chest", containing gems of wisdom summarizing salient points in the story and challenging the children to reflect and think.

Of course, there are no rigid standards as to what is "best" in this world. Everyone has his own standards. The stories chosen are based on criteria stated above. If you have a good story that fits these criteria, and you think it should be included, please submit it to us. If your story is chosen and published, your name will be acknowledged and you will receive part of any forthcoming royalties.

Dr. Robert Chi-Kwong Lee

Table of Contents

The Cunning Sun-Tze 1

Su-Su, the Wise Young Bride 6

The Man Who Was "The Best in The Land" 11

Wu and the Magnificent Golden Stallion...........19

The Man Who Came Back From Heaven..........25

Mr. Tsai Lost His Horse.....................................31

The Swallow and the Sparrow 38

The First Lie-Detector.......................................46

THE CUNNING SUN-TZE

Background:

Sun-Tze was one of the most famous generals in China. Although he was born approximately 2500 years ago, he is still considered one of the foremost military strategists of all time. His book, The Art of War, has been translated into many languages and is taught in both military academies and business schools throughout the world. He is most famous for his unconventional thinking. This story illustrates one of his methods.

When Sun-Tze was just a young boy, he and his best friend Peng, went to find a teacher to instruct them in wisdom and the "art of war," or military strategy. In old China, there were no schools. Everyone had to find his own teacher, who was called "*Shi fu*", meaning "Teacher-father". Peng was several years older than Sun-Tze, but the two were as close as brothers. When they arrived at the teacher's house, the teacher met them at the door.

"I will take you as my students, if you can pass this test," said the *Shi fu*, looking at the boys' eager faces. "I am inside the house now. If you can find a way to get me out of my house then I will accept you."

"Oh, that's easy," boasted the older Peng. "I'll set fire to your house and you will have to get out." Peng put his hands on his hips and looked the *Shi fu* boldly in the eye.

The *Shi fu* gazed at Peng thoughtfully. "Yes. That's rather cruel, though." Peng shuffled his feet uneasily under the *Shi fu*'s steady gaze. The *Shi fu* paused for a long time. "Nevertheless, it works," he said at last. "You pass. You may be my student. " Peng breathed a sigh of relief and grinned triumphantly.

Then the *Shi fu* turned to young Sun-Tze, who was deep in thought. "How about you, little boy?"

"Well," said Sun-Tze slowly, "I can't think of a better way to get you out of the house. However, I thought of an absolutely marvelous and most ingenious way of getting you back into the house once you are outside."

"Really?" said the *Shi fu*, intrigued. "All right, show me," he said, stepping out of the house.

"Thank you, sir! I just passed," replied Sun-Tze with a shy smile.

The *Shi fu* laughed and laughed. "Ah, yes!" he clapped his hands together. "You are very clever! I will enjoy teaching you, indeed! To be able to win without violence and to conquer without fighting is the way of a true general. You will go far."

Postscript: Because of Sun-Tze's talent, the teacher loved him and taught him everything he knew. Peng became very jealous and turned against his friend, becoming an archenemy who created much trouble for Sun-Tze later. Do you want to know more about the adventures of Sun-Tze? More to come!

TREASURE CHEST:

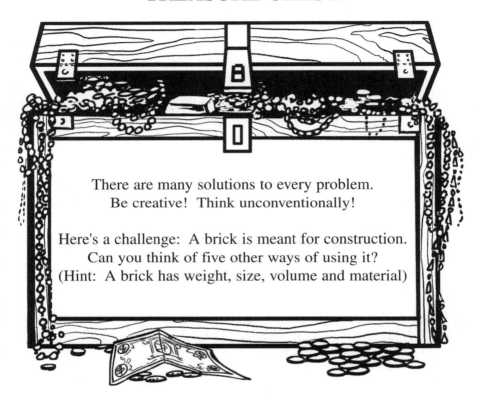

There are many solutions to every problem.
Be creative! Think unconventionally!

Here's a challenge: A brick is meant for construction.
Can you think of five other ways of using it?
(Hint: A brick has weight, size, volume and material)

SU SU, THE WISE YOUNG BRIDE

Background:

In ancient China, there was no government-run social security, as we know in the U.S. When people grew old, the business was always passed on to the eldest son. The household power and duties would then be passed on to the eldest son's wife. This way, the old folks would be well taken care of by the younger people.

Big news! Number one son was getting married!

It was big news indeed. The oldest son of the Lee family was marrying a young bride from the Chen family. The young bride, Su Su, was both beautiful and capable. Her painting and embroidery were both outstanding. She was also wise and gentle. Everyone loved her. She was polite to elders and kind to the servants.

Her mother-in-law was indeed very proud to have such a wonderful daughter-in-law to take over the household when that time came. She was busy training Su Su about all the household duties.

"You are so efficient, Ma!" remarked Su Su one day. "You know everything! I wish that I could do half as well."

"You are very smart, Su Su," Mother-in-law Lee beamed with pride, patting Su Su's back. "Just follow my example closely and you will do just fine."

One day, Su Su was walking in the garden. She came upon Grandma Lee who was sitting under a tree and crying quietly. Su Su frowned with concern and quietly approached the old woman.

"Why are you so sad, Grandma Lee?" she asked gently.

"I am getting old, Su Su," Grandma Lee sighed, quickly wiping her eyes. "Ever since Grandpa died, your mother-in-law has not allowed me to sit at the family table. Every meal, I am only allowed a meager ration of food in this rice bowl. I have not had a decent meal since Grandpa died! Perhaps it is better to die!" Grandma Lee began to sob.

"Nonsense," said Su Su, gently patting the old woman's bent back. "I will help you, Grandma

Lee." She thought for a minute, then bent low to whisper in the old woman's ear. "When you come to dinner tonight, drop your rice bowl and be sure to break it. I will help you."

"Oh, no!" exclaimed Grandma Lee, her eyes wide with fright. "Your mother-in-law will kill me!"

"Do as I say, dear Grandma, and your troubles will be over," assured Su Su with a smile, and with that, she quietly continued her walk.

That night at dinnertime, Grandma Lee promptly dropped her bowl and broke it. The mother-in-law was furious! But before anyone could say a word, Su Su jumped up and pointed her finger at Grandma Lee, pretending to be very angry.

"How dare you break that traditional rice bowl!" Su Su scolded. "Now what is mother going to use when she gets old?"

Suddenly, the mother-in-law realized the error of her ways. "Aiyaa! What sort of example have I set for Su Su?" she thought to herself with alarm. She did not want to be treated the way she was treating

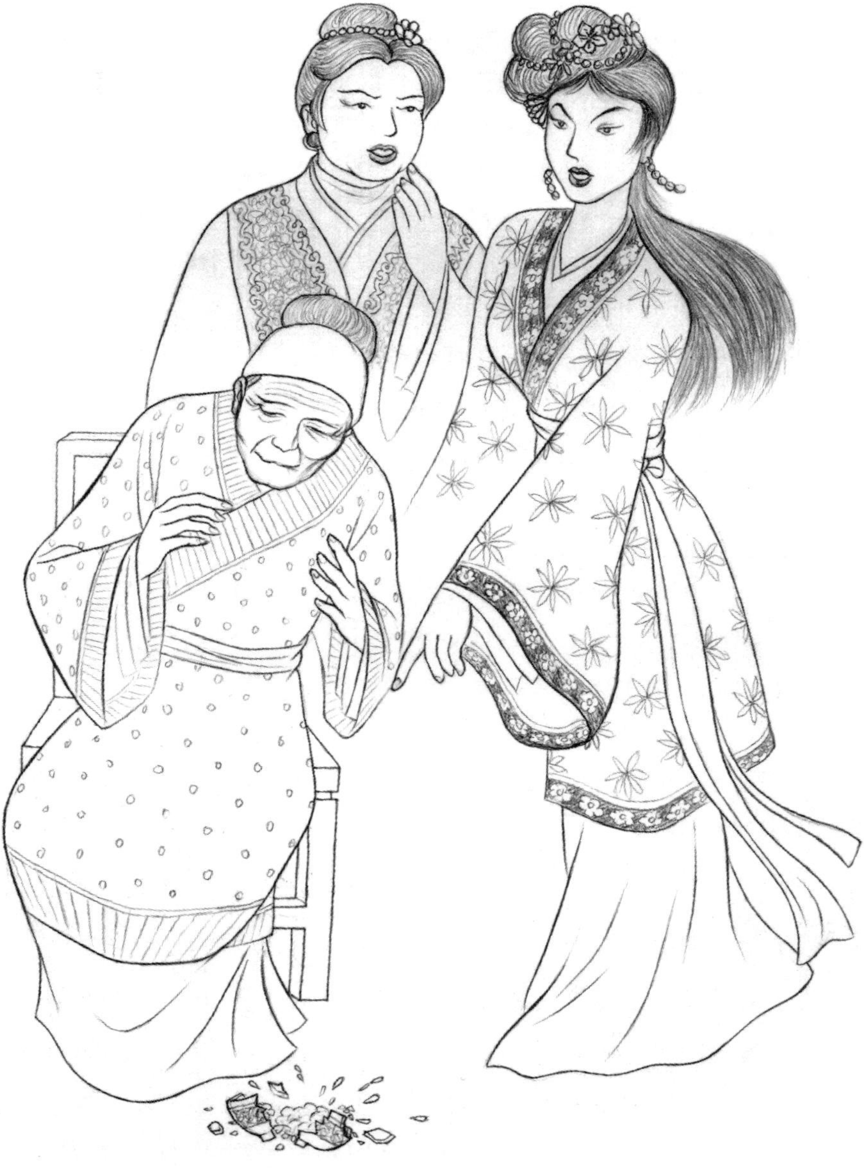

Grandma Lee when she herself grew old!

From that day on, Grandma Lee was invited to sit at the family table in a place of honor and respect, and the whole family lived in harmony for many years.

TREASURE CHEST:

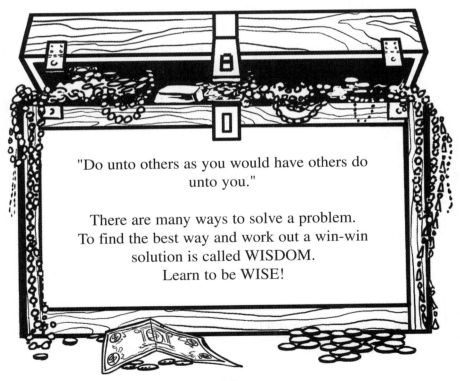

"Do unto others as you would have others do unto you."

There are many ways to solve a problem.
To find the best way and work out a win-win solution is called WISDOM.
Learn to be WISE!

THE MAN WHO WAS
"THE BEST IN THE LAND"

Once there was a kind, young farmer named Han. He was very poor and could not afford to take a wife, and indeed most of the women in town did not want to marry someone so poor. One day, the father of his distant cousin, Mei, died suddenly and left her with nothing. Mei was not much to look at but she was well educated and very capable. Han did not want to let her just fend for herself, for in old China there were no opportunities for single women, and in fact, it could be dangerous for them. So, Han asked Mei to marry him, and she agreed.

Han and Mei worked side by side, and Han was surprised at the difference it made for his small farm! With his wife's capable management, Han's farm soon became very successful and productive. Han was amazed! The animals were thriving. In fact, soon Han's pigs were the biggest and the fattest in the country. After a number of years, Han actually became prosperous.

Then Mei advised Han to use the extra money to buy a cloth factory, and soon, her wise management and Han's hard work began to produce the best silk in the land. Mei also suggested that Han invest in a winery, and soon their partnership began to produce the best wines!

Unfortunately, as Han became more and more prosperous, he became more and more proud. Soon he began bragging among the city elders that he was simply "the best in the land" at everything; he produced the best wines, the best silks and the biggest farm animals --nothing was too difficult for him. The elders rolled their eyes and grew tired of Han's never-ending bragging. Soon they began to complain to each other about Han, and they even complained to the governor of the city.

When the governor heard about Han's bragging, he determined to teach him a lesson. He sent an official summons addressed to "Han, The Best in the Land." Han's chest swelled with pride when he received the official document.

"I really am the Best in the Land! Even the governor says so," said Han smugly as he promptly went to see the governor.

As Han approached the governor's mansion, he admired himself in the governor's long reflecting pools. He saw the beautiful silk paintings on the governor's wall, and told himself they must be made with silk from his factory. He could smell the aroma of roast pork wafting from the governor's kitchen, and imagined that it was probably a pig raised on his farm. No doubt, the governor will even serve me some of my own wine, he sighed to himself. Han was positively beaming with confidence when he finally stood before the governor.

"Greetings Han. I understand you have been telling everybody you are the best in the land!" said the governor. "Is this true?"

"Well, sir, I do produce the best pigs in the land-- and the best silk, and the best wine," said Han, smiling to himself.

"And the city elders tell me that you say nothing is too hard for you, is that correct?" asked the governor.

Han was feeling very proud now. "Well, that could be, that could be," he said, smiling happily.

Perhaps the governor is going to give me a special award of honor, he thought to himself.

"Well, then, it should be easy for you to help us with a few requests," said the governor. "I would like you to do the following: 1) raise a pig as big as a mountain; 2) make enough wine to fill the ocean and 3) make cloth as long as the road that goes across China. That is all, you may go."

Han's face fell. He quickly stammered his goodbye and stumbled out of the governor's office. "Oh no, what have I done?" he wailed as he hurried past the long reflecting pools. "These are impossible tasks! And yet, I cannot refuse the governor! I will be the laughing stock of the whole town, disgraced in front of everybody! What shall I do?"

Han trudged home and confided his troubles to Mei, but she just smiled. "Don't worry, Han," she said. "Tomorrow, you must go back to the governor with three things: a scale, a measuring bucket and a yardstick."

Han looked at her, incredulously. "What good will that do?" he asked, his stomach still churning with

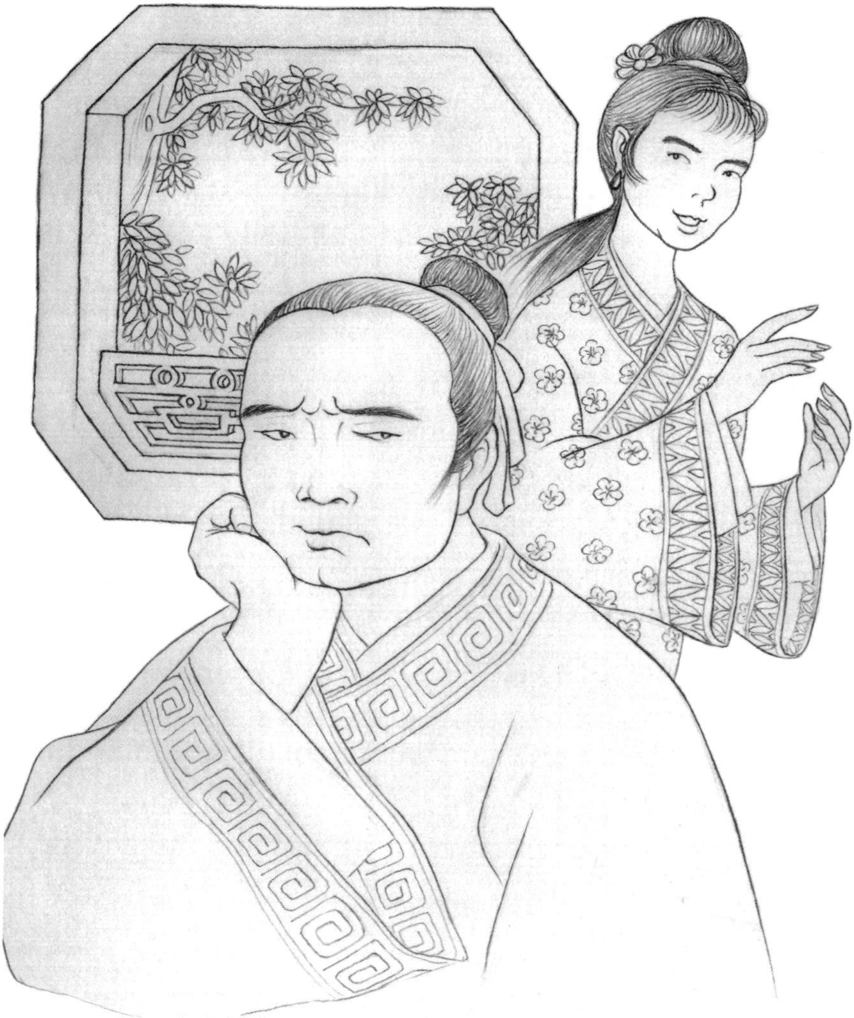

worry.

"Ask the governor to weigh the mountain so that you will know how big the pig must be, to measure the ocean and tell you how many gallons you will need and to measure the road to see how long the cloth must be," answered Mei calmly.

The next day Han went back to the governor and did just that. The governor was very impressed with the wit and cleverness of Han, who had suddenly turned the tables on him! Yet, the governor could tell that Han was a simple man, for a clever one would not have been bragging in the first place.

"Tell me, Han, how is it that you were so distressed with these tasks yesterday, and today you have these very clever answers for me?" asked the governor.

Han hung his head. "I cannot pretend to be that clever, sir," he admitted. "It is my wife who is the clever one. She is the one who told me what to say. In fact, she is the one who has taught me everything. It is her good management and ideas and my hard work that has made our businesses successful. By myself, I was only a poor farmer--the poorest in the whole city!"

The governor smiled. "It takes a wise man to admit his weaknesses and tell the truth, Han. Never mind about the demands I made of you. Instead, I would like to meet your wife. I think she may have some clever solutions to the problems of the whole city!"

With that, Mei began to consult with the governor and the city officials on a regular basis. Soon the entire province became very prosperous, based on Mei's wise ideas and everybody's hard work.

TREASURE CHEST:

Bragging always causes trouble!
Pride goes before a fall,
but humility reveals wisdom.

If you are in trouble, get help.

Han really needed Mei to be successful. But
Mei needed Han, too. Can you figure out why?

WU AND THE MAGNIFICENT GOLDEN STALLION

Wu was a young stable boy in the household of an important official. He was in charge of the master's prize stallion. This was a magnificent horse. It was very fast, very strong and very beautiful. Wu called the horse Golden Stallion because of the way its beautiful coat gleamed in the bright sun. He loved the horse and Golden Stallion loved him too. When Wu would brush the underside of the horse's neck, Golden Stallion would raise his front legs and neigh.

Wu had to exercise the horse every morning. Round and round the fenced-in yard they went. Wu often wondered just how fast Golden Stallion could run. He often imagined that he was a fearless warrior charging into battle with his mighty horse. Unfortunately the master had forbidden Wu to race the horse for fear that the horse would get hurt.

One day, early in the morning, Wu's opportunity finally came. "Wu!" bellowed the Master. "Take this document to Governor Lee in the capitol. It's urgent - you must get there as fast as possible!

Take the stallion!"

Wu couldn't believe his ears. "The - the stallion?" he stammered.

"Go, boy! There is no time to lose!" thundered the Master, and Wu was off!

As soon as he left the house, he put the horse into full gallop. He felt like the king's best knight charging into battle to save a captive princess! On and on, he rode, the wind streaming through his hair. Wu imagined he charged right into the middle of the enemy camp.

"Take this! Take that!" he cried, waving his imaginary sword. "Don't worry, princess, I will save you!" as he scooped up his pretend princess. "Oh, no!" said Wu, imagining enemy archers all around him. "Do your trick now, Golden Stallion, save us!"

Golden Stallion leaped up so high that Wu thought he was in heaven! The horse's mane flashed in the sunlight as the two raced across the countryside. For hours they rode without stopping.

It was late afternoon when Wu finally arrived at his destination. Governor Lee gave Wu something to eat and ordered him to wait for the reply to his master. It was almost evening when Wu left for home. Soon the night turned dark and cold as it does in northern China at that time of year. Wu regretted that he had forgotten his jacket when he left in such a hurry. Before long, he began to shiver in the cold and he turned the horse toward a nearby inn.

The next morning, Wu got up at dawn, eager to resume his journey home. But when he went to the stable, Golden Stallion was gone! In his place stood an old skinny horse that was blind in one eye. The animal was indeed a sorry sight to behold. Wu ran back to the inn and confronted the innkeeper.

"Where is my horse?" demanded Wu, his voice filling with both anger and panic.

"Now, now, young sir. I am not responsible for any losses," insisted the innkeeper. "The merchant who checked out earlier must have taken your horse instead of his own. He did not leave his name or address."

"Oh no! My master will kill me," wailed Wu, fighting back tears. "I could never go home without the horse! What will I do? He will kill me!"

"Ah, there now. You are only a young boy," said the innkeeper, taking pity on poor Wu. "I'll tell you what. There is an old sage in the town. Perhaps he will be able to help you." Wu rubbed the tears from his eyes and followed the innkeeper's directions to find the old sage.

The old sage was wrinkled from head to toe, and his thin white beard fell all the way to the floor. But the sage's eyes were kind, and he listened patiently to Wu's tale of woe. He asked if the boy had any money.

"A little," said Wu, furiously rubbing back his tears.

"Go to the store and buy a basket of salt and feed it to the old horse, but don't give him any water," said the sage. "After one hour, get on the old horse. Let him go wherever he pleases and you will find your horse."

Wu did not understand how the old sage's advice would help, but he did as he was told. He fed the horse the salt, waited an hour, and got on the old horse's back. Soon the old horse started to trot, gathered up speed and then ran as if a demon were on his tail! Wu held on tight, for he had no idea where they were headed. After some time, the horse jumped over a low fence and dove right into a big water trough! Sure enough, right next to the water trough was Golden Stallion!

The old sage knew that when a horse is thirsty, its

one all consuming thought is to return home for water. And a horse can always find its way home!

TREASURE CHEST:

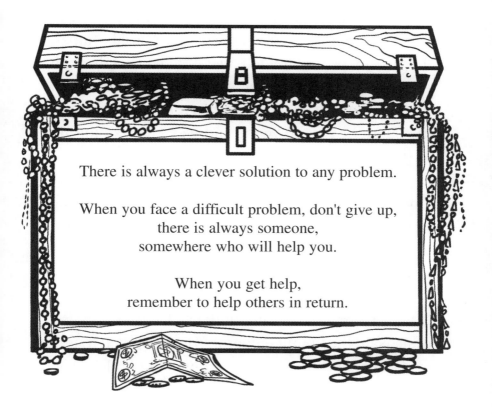

There is always a clever solution to any problem.

When you face a difficult problem, don't give up,
there is always someone,
somewhere who will help you.

When you get help,
remember to help others in return.

THE MAN WHO CAME BACK
FROM HEAVEN

Some time ago in China, the emperor passed away and the young prince took over the duties of ruling the kingdom. The emperor left the prince two of his most trusted aides: the builder who had built the emperor's palaces and cities, and an artist who decorated them. Being very devoted to his father, the young prince treated these two officials with great respect and honor. Unbeknownst to him, though, the artist had grown increasingly jealous of the builder over the years, and was always plotting to get the better of him.

One day, a king from a foreign country visited the young emperor. "Oh, what a magnificent palace you have. There is nothing like it on this earth!" said the visiting king.

"Oh, it is the work of my builder. He is simply the best," said the young emperor. He continued to talk of the wonderful palaces and cities the builder had built.

The artist was standing nearby, listening to the

emperor praise the builder. As the emperor went on, without a word about the artist's work, the artist became very jealous and resentful. "I simply have to get rid of that builder. Then I'll finally get all the glory and praise!" he muttered to himself.

One day, the artist thought of a very devious scheme. He took an old parchment and drew strange symbols and writings on it, and had his servant present it to the emperor, saying that it fell from heaven. Since no one from the court could read what it said, the emperor asked the artist where it came from.

"Oh, this is from your father," exclaimed the artist, pretending to be surprised. "He says he is very happy in heaven. He wants to build a palace there but there are no good builders. He has asked you to send him your builder. Once the palace is built, he will send him back. Here is how you do it. You will build a tower and place firewood all around it. Have the builder sit in the middle of the fire. He will quickly ascend to your father and your father will return him safely as soon as the new palace is built," concluded the artist. "So says the parchment," he added quickly.

Being very devoted to his father, the emperor ordered the builder to go to heaven following those instructions.

"Oh, Great Emperor, I will be happy to go. Merely give me 30 days to build the tower and set my affairs in order," said the builder, knowing full well that this was a murderous trick of the artist.

During that month, the builder built the special tower. On top of the tower was a chair mounted on a marble slab. Under the slab, and known only to the builder, was a secret tunnel that led directly to the basement of his house.

When the day came, the builder sat on the chair. All the top officials and the emperor were there to give him a great send-off. The builder instructed his family to weep bitterly in front of the emperor, and the emperor showered them with many gifts, including money equal to ten years of the builder's salary.

Soon the guards lit the bonfire, and as the smoke curled upward, the builder raised his hands as if to

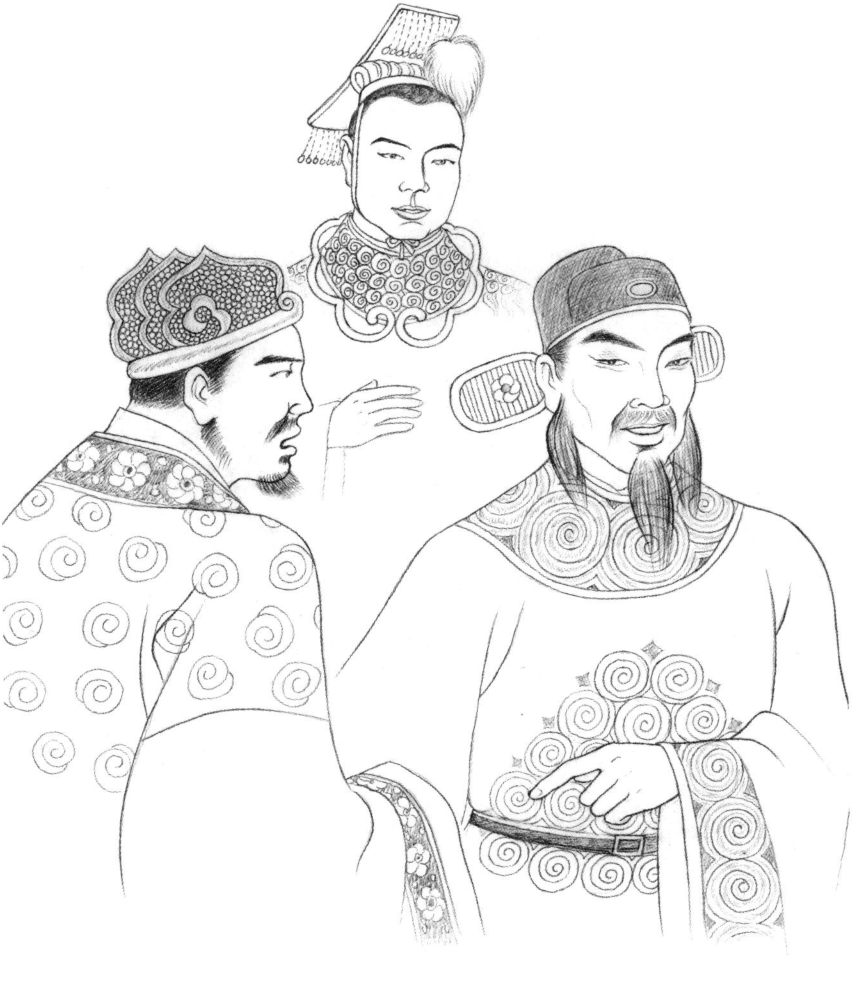

ascend to heaven. The smoke grew into a thick, dark cloud that closed over his head and out-stretched hands. As the smoke hid him from view, the builder quickly crawled under the slab, replaced it carefully and escaped to safety.

After the fire subsided, they found the burned chair but no trace of the body. The artist smiled and imagined how he would enjoy having a place of honor all to himself.

Three months later, the builder reappeared to the emperor in a strange white robe that he had pre-pared. All of the emperor's court bowed low with respect and fear. Here was a man that actually returned from heaven! The artist's jaw dropped in shock and horror.

"Oh, Great Emperor," called out the builder. "The palace is built and your father is overjoyed. All he needs now is to have the palace decorated." The builder turned his gaze calmly to the horrified artist. "He asks that you please send up his favorite artist at once in the same manner."

The emperor's court erupted in applause and clamored around the artist, joyfully encouraging him to go outside to the waiting tower.

And that was the end of the artist and his jealous and evil schemes.

TREASURE CHEST:

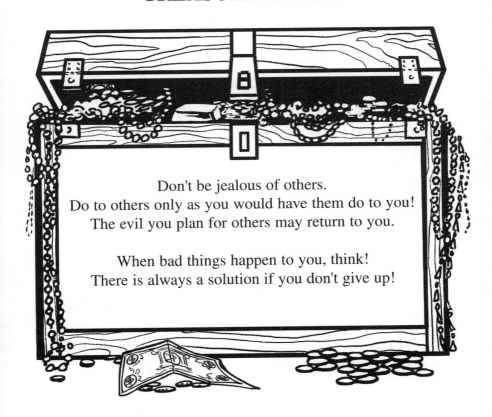

Don't be jealous of others.
Do to others only as you would have them do to you!
The evil you plan for others may return to you.

When bad things happen to you, think!
There is always a solution if you don't give up!

MR. TSAI LOST HIS HORSE

Background:

This story is based on a Chinese proverb that is ages old. As you may or may not know, a Chinese proverb consists of precisely four words, usually based on a story illustrating a specific point. This story has been told and retold countless times, often with a different twist each time. See if you can retell this story, adding your own ideas and imagination!

Once upon a time, there was a farmer and rancher named Mr. Tsai. He was not very wealthy, but he was gentle, kind, and very wise. Every morning he would walk to the marketplace to discuss the day's affairs with the other villagers. Everyone in his village liked and respected him.

One morning, while Mr. Tsai was in the marketplace, his son Ping rushed up to him, very upset. "Papa, our prized white stallion is gone! This careless servant forgot to lock the gate!" Ping pointed an accusing finger at the stable boy, Li, who trudged up behind him, his head bowed low in despair.

"Forgive me master, the gate was broken late last night," said Li, dejectedly. "I tried to repair it as well as I could in the dark, but the powerful white stallion just kicked it open and ran away! Please forgive me!" Li knelt in the dust before Mr. Tsai, knowing that the loss of the stallion might well cost him his job.

"He was the best horse we ever had! There was none like him for miles around -he was priceless, Papa," insisted Ping, crossing his arms. "This is very bad! Li must pay - or be severely punished!"

By now, a large crowd of concerned villagers had gathered around the troubled threesome. "Oh yes, it is very bad that you lost your wonderful white stallion, Mr. Tsai," echoed everyone in the village, shaking their heads and looking down at the unfortunate servant, Li.

"Ah well, it is not necessarily bad," replied Mr. Tsai. He held out his hand to help Li get up off his knees and quietly forgave him.

The next day, the white stallion came back and brought with him ten wild horses. One stallion was a beautiful color, as golden as the sun, and clearly both strong and spirited. Ping rejoiced as he saw the horses come into the ranch and rushed to the marketplace to tell his father.

"Papa, Papa, we are rich! You must look at the golden stallion! What a majestic war horse he will make. He will easily be worth a thousand pieces of gold!" exclaimed Ping. "I will try to break him in tomorrow and sell him to the general!"

"Oh, congratulations, Mr. Tsai! This is indeed very good for you," applauded everyone in the village.

"Oh, it is not necessarily good," countered Mr. Tsai, with a smile.

Sure enough, the next day, Ping got up early and eagerly ordered Li to saddle up the golden stallion. "Wow! Look at him!" murmured Ping, as Li struggled to put a saddle on the wild horse. The golden stallion reared up on its powerful hind legs, trying to shake off the saddle and reins. Ping imagined the stallion charging into battle with the same power and fierceness. "This horse is worth its weight in gold!" Ping marveled, as he mounted the wild horse.

Ping began to think of all the money he would get for the horse, and all he would be able to buy as a result. Suddenly, the horse bucked violently and threw Ping to the ground. A searing pain went through Ping's leg. Li rushed to his side and then summoned the best doctor in town, but it was no use. Ping became permanently crippled.

"Oh, that's too bad, Mr. Tsai. He is your only son!" the sympathetic villagers exclaimed when they heard the news.

"Well..." sighed Mr. Tsai slowly, "it's not necessarily bad."

A few months later, the general came to town and drafted all the able-bodied young men to fight in the civil war.

"Ping must come too even though he is a cripple," said the general. "He will make a good cook!"

"I'll give you something a thousand times better than a crippled boy," said Mr. Tsai to the general, leading him to the stables. "Li, bring out the golden stallion!" ordered Mr. Tsai. Li brought out the spirited golden stallion, who had been tamed in the months since Ping's accident.

"Now, General, is this not the most wonderful war horse you have ever seen?" said Mr. Tsai. "He could save your life in a battle!"

The general was delighted, and agreed to leave Ping and take the golden stallion immediately. In no time at all, he and the new recruits rode off to the war front. As it turned out, many of those young men were killed in the battle, and never returned.

Many months later, Ping sat on the porch with his father, after attending yet another funeral for one of the young men who had gone with the general. "Wow, that was close, Papa," mused Ping, quietly. "Who would have thought that a little broken gate might actually lead to saving my life one day?"

"Yes, my son, life is like that," said Mr. Tsai. "Good things are not necessarily good and bad things are not necessarily bad. If we live our life with honesty and love for our fellow men, we will have a satisfying and long life."

Sure enough, Mr. Tsai lived a long and happy life with Ping and many grandchildren, in perfect harmony with his neighbors.

TREASURE CHEST:

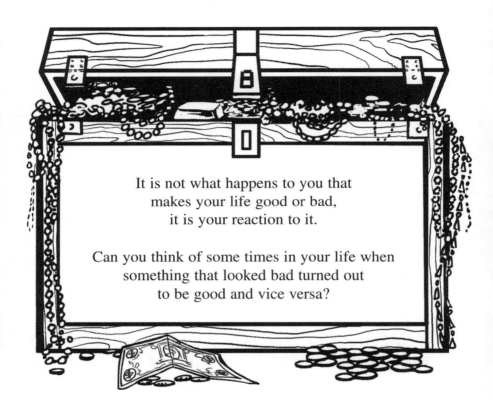

It is not what happens to you that
makes your life good or bad,
it is your reaction to it.

Can you think of some times in your life when
something that looked bad turned out
to be good and vice versa?

THE SWALLOW AND THE SPARROW

"The Yentzes (Chinese for swallow) are coming home again," Mother Sparrow said as she heard the church bells ring.

"Really, is it March already? My, my!" marveled Father Sparrow.

"Who are the Yentzes?" asked their young son, Junior.

"They are swallows, a different kind of bird. They come back every year in the spring and leave in the fall. They don't stay here all year round like us sparrows," said Father Sparrow.

"Where are they coming from?" asked Junior, hopping from one leg to the other.

"I understand that they came from their home down south, some 10,000 miles away," said Father Sparrow.

"Wow! That is a long way. Why do they leave? Don't they know that there is lots of food here all year round?" asked Junior.

"I don't know, Son, why don't you ask them?" sighed Father Sparrow, tiring of his son's endless questions.

"I will, I will ask them tomorrow!" said Junior, his bright eyes sparkling with excitement.

The next day, two black shadows glided in silently and landed in the eaves. Kwong (meaning Light) and Mei (meaning Beauty) got busy right away cleaning up their nest. They were swift and grace-ful with tails like long scissors.

Early the next morning, Junior hopped over to see Kwong. "Dad told me that you came a long way. Is that true?"

"Yes, we flew over 10,000 miles, over mountains and oceans," answered Kwong.

"Wow, what's the ocean like? I've never been there!" exclaimed Junior, his eyes wide with wonder.

"Oh, it's beautiful! And it's only a few miles from here!" chuckled Kwong.

"Awww, my mom and dad won't let me fly anywhere far from here," scowled Junior. "Besides, they say there are hawks there! Aren't you afraid of the hawks?"

"No, they can never catch us," said Kwong proudly. "We deliberately play 'catch me if you can' with them sometimes. We fly close to them and taunt them. They get mad and chase us but we are much faster than they are!"

Kwong suddenly tilted his head, listened intently and then shot off like a dart. Soon he came back with a grasshopper in his mouth. He caught it in mid-air and gave it to Mei who was busy laying eggs.

"Wow, how did you do that?" Junior was very impressed. "You must teach me how to do that!"

"Sure, come back tomorrow," smiled Kwong, winking at Mei.

Junior could hardly sleep that night. "I am going to learn to be a swallow tomorrow," Junior whispered to himself. "I am tired of being just a sparrow! Hop! Hop! Hop!"

Early the next morning, Junior caught a fat juicy worm and gathered some of the best tasting seeds and brought them all to Kwong as presents. Kwong thanked him politely and put them aside.

"Now, lesson one is: listen," said Kwong to his young student. "There are a grasshopper and a dragonfly nearby. Can you hear them? Can you hear their distinct sounds?"

"No, I can't hear a thing!" said Junior, straining his ears.

"Watch!" commanded Kwong, as he leaped off, quickly returned with a dragonfly and fed it to Mei who was nesting on the eggs.

"Wow!" said Junior admiringly, "Teach me how to do that!"

"Okay! See if you can follow me," said Kwong.

Junior spent all morning chasing after Kwong. He had never noticed so many flying insects in his life. Kwong was having a ball dining on his smorgasbord. But try as he might, Junior could hardly catch even one. Finally frustrated and exhausted, Junior sat panting.

"Why don't you eat something," said Kwong.

"Take the worm and seeds."

"No, no, they are presents for you," said Junior, smoothing his aching wings dejectedly.

"You know, we appreciate that," said Kwong, gently. "But, you see, swallows are built for speed. We have very strong wings but small and weak legs. We can't hop and catch worms like you do, so we eat only flying insects from the air. We cannot digest seeds at all. To fly fast, our feathers are not thick like yours, which means they also cannot protect us through the winter."

"So that's why you fly south every October?" asked Junior.

"Yes. Another reason is that there are fewer flying insects after the harvest."

"Wow, that must be hard work, flying thousands of miles," said Junior, remembering how exhausted he was after just one hour of near-constant flying.

"It's not that bad for a swallow," said Kwong. "We were designed to do that. Just as you were designed to be able to stay right here."

That night, Junior returned home tired but happy.

"Hello, little 'Swallow'," said Father Sparrow, grinning at his exhausted little son. "How did it go?"

"Aww, Dad! Do you know that swallows can't hop? They can't eat worms and seeds and they have to fly for hours just to catch their food? Plus their feathers are so thin, they can't keep them warm enough to stay here for the winter!" said Junior. "They are fast, but not carefree like us sparrows! I think I'll go out to a tree and sing!" announced Junior, and he hopped proudly out of his house. Hop! Hop! Hop!

TREASURE CHEST:

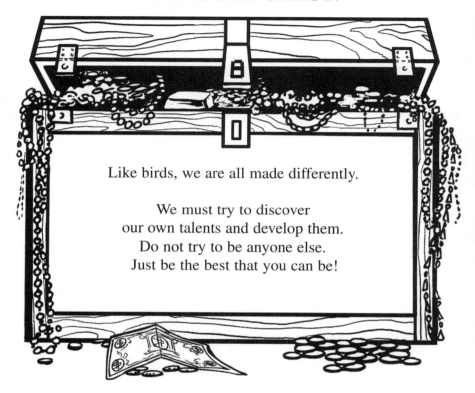

Like birds, we are all made differently.

We must try to discover
our own talents and develop them.
Do not try to be anyone else.
Just be the best that you can be!

As this little poem says:

Each morning when you rise,
Light up your spark of divine fire.
It matters little that you win or lose,
Just to your own self, be true!

-- from "Marathon", RCK Lee

THE FIRST LIE-DETECTOR
(The Mayor and the Sacred Bell)

Background:

In old China, there were no judges. The mayor of each city judged all disputes and crimes in his area.

One night in old China, a robbery occurred in the house of Mr. Chang, a high government official. Mr. Chang and everyone in the house was killed and the house was set on fire. It was a vicious and terrible crime, and it shook the whole country. The Emperor was enraged and was determined to find the criminals. He ordered that the case must be solved in ninety days or someone --either the police chief or the mayor-- would lose his head!

Since there were no eyewitnesses and the house was burned to the ground, this became a very difficult case. The police could find no clues. The cruelty of the attack, however, made the police suspect some of the worst criminals in China. Some of them had been angry with Mr. Chang for one reason or another. The police rounded up twelve possible suspects but they all claimed to be innocent. Since there were no lie detectors in those days, there was no way to find out who was telling the truth. The police were certain, however, that one or more of the men was guilty.

The police brought the case before Mayor Chen, who was a rather young mayor, but known to be very clever. Mayor Chen looked sternly at the twelve suspects standing before him, and listened as the police stated their case, including their unfortunate lack of proof. The suspects all looked very smug and cocky as they stared back boldly at the Mayor.

Mayor Chen looked thoughtful. "This is indeed a difficult case, officers. We will have to look to the most special and sacred of tools to help us. Fortunately, I have just the thing." Mayor Chen clapped his hands quickly and turned to his assistants. "Bring in the Sacred Bell."

Immediately, the mayor's assistants scurried out and returned pushing a heavy red cart. On the cart was a huge, bell-shaped item covered with a thick veil of black velvet. On one side of the bell there were two slits in the veil, each just big enough to fit a man's hand. On the other side, a small golden tube protruded from the folds of fabric. Incense burners on the cart further covered the mysterious bell in a billowing cloud of incense. The police officers and the suspects were very curious, and a little afraid.

"Behold the Sacred Bell of China!" announced Mayor Chen. "Confucius himself brought this bell down from the Temple of the Three Heavenly Peaks. No one may look upon its unveiled form, for it is pure and should not be exposed to the common air here in the valleys. However, its purity gives the Sacred Bell miraculous powers. Anyone who has a guilty and impure heart and touches it will cause such a disturbance in its purity that the bell will vibrate with pain to announce the person's guilt."

"Now, I want each of you, one by one, to pronounce your claim of innocence and then place your hands inside the veil to touch the bell. I will listen through the golden tube to detect the bell's vibration. It will tell me who is guilty and who is innocent. The Sacred Bell does not lie."

With the blowing of the trumpet and rolling of the drums, the suspects approached the bell one by one. Mayor Chen watched carefully as each one said, "I am innocent of the attack on Mr. Chang and his household. May the Sacred Bell speak truth." Then the mayor put his ear to the golden tube and listened for the secret vibration. One criminal went up, then another one. Nobody could hear the bell's vibration but Mayor Chen, and his face remained stern and unchanged. When the last suspect had gone through the test, the Mayor lined all the men up once again.

"These three are your guilty ones. Arrest them to await their punishment!" announced Mayor Chen. The three men wailed and hung their heads, and quickly confessed to everything.

Question: How did Mayor Chen know? Do you think the Sacred Bell really had magical powers? (See Solution on page 52)

TREASURE CHEST:

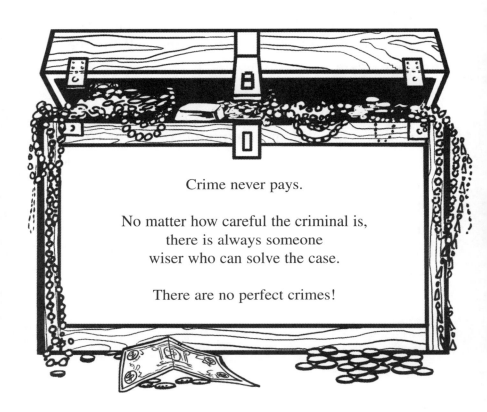

Crime never pays.

No matter how careful the criminal is,
there is always someone
wiser who can solve the case.

There are no perfect crimes!

****

Solution: The Mayor covered the outside of the bell with charcoal dust before he put the black veil over it. While he pretended to be busy listening, he was actually examining the hands of the suspects as they took their hands away from touching the bell. The innocent ones were unafraid to touch it, and their hands came away covered with charcoal dust. The guilty ones had clean hands because they had just gone through the motions, never daring to actually touch the bell lest it sound!

****